The Chalk Girl of Little India

Written by John Parsons
Illustrated by Pat Reynolds

Contents

For learning solutions, visit cengage.com.au

Meet the Characters

Navita

A chalk girl.

Rajaratnam

Navita's uncle,
a master tailor.

The Client

A foreign traveller.

Author's note: In this story, you will see Rajaratnam's shop is called Rajaratnam S/O Govindarajan. In Singapore, "S/O" is a common abbreviation that means "son of". Although it is not as common, "D/O" means "daughter of". These abbreviations are used to show that a business has been owned and run by many generations of a family.

Dear Reader

I love travelling to Singapore. It is a colourful, friendly and culturally diverse island full of fascinating places and people. Last time I was there, I went to Little India, where lots of tailors offered to make me a suit. Normally, I would have said "yes", but it was so hot I could hardly wear a t-shirt, let alone a suit! Maybe next time I'll go during the cooler monsoon months!

John Parsons
Author

Singapore

1. The island of Singapore
2. Little India (a suburb of the city)
3. Malaysia
4. The Merlion: half lion, half sea creature, and the symbol of Singapore

1 Little India

There was barely a cloud in the Singapore sky. Under the relentless afternoon sun, the canopies and awnings that adorned the laneways and alleys of Little India offered little respite from the October temperatures. The heat built up, as if daring the monsoon season to come early and break its hold on the city and its people.

In this district of the island, luscious saris the colour of ripe mandarins and plums, and bright headscarves flecked with strands of gold thread flapped restlessly from garment racks in the street. Rows of tiny carved elephants and brigades of plastic Hindu gods watched over columns of gold bangles, each stall a kaleidoscope of colour and culture. The sounds of bicycle bells and car horns, and the smells of spices and incense filled the humid, sticky air.

Morning trade had been good. But by four o'clock, the hawk-eyed traders who darted from customer to customer sensed that the tourists were wilting, abandoning the two-storey shophouses of Little India for the air-conditioned comforts of the boutiques lining Orchard Road or the cafes of Clarke Quay. As the afternoon trade slowed, they too retreated inside their stalls to swig gulps of water from the bottles they used to lure customers inside.

Navita hurried past the gold traders of Serangoon Road, a bundle of tightly wrapped fabric under her arm. She slipped into a laneway, one of four that wound themselves together in a covered market. Trapped by the stalls on either side, the half-hearted breezes of Serangoon Road carried no relief, only the heat of the afternoon, deep into the market. She ran between the groups of tailors and hawkers regaling each other with recounts of the morning's trade. At the intersection of the laneways, she turned left. Navita followed that laneway outside to her destination.

"Rajaratnam S/O Govindarajan" announced the sign over the shophouse's door. It was a long name, as long as the tradition of tailoring that its owner, Navita's uncle Rajaratnam, had proudly followed since her grandfather Govindarajan began the business in 1964. "Master Tailors and Alterations for Distinguished Gentlemen. Finest Suits in Two Days. Worldwide Shipping."

A bell tinkled as Navita opened the pale green door. Rajaratnam, who was sitting behind a desk crowded with receipts and order slips, barely looked up. He was tearing a *bhatura* into bite-size pieces, slowly chewing the flatbread as he worked.

"*Madhiya vanakkam*, Uncle," murmured Navita as she walked past. "Good afternoon."

Rajaratnam glanced up. "*Madhiya vanakkam*," he replied. Formal greetings were always used behind the pale green door of Rajaratnam S/O Govindarajan. "Tradition and formality," Rajaratnam had said when Navita was first employed, "are essential in the front room."

"Properness," he called it. "My clients expect nothing less than properness." Navita wasn't sure that was even a word, but she followed Rajaratnam's wishes. He was the owner and a master tailor who could make fine suits for distinguished gentlemen in only two days. She was just a chalk girl who worked after school, marking out where the fabric should be cut to start sewing the morning's orders. Her other job was to carry the cut panels of fabric upstairs, where Ovashni the seamstress expertly sewed them together, and to bring the finished suits downstairs. But, when a client was in the front room, she was never allowed to speak.

"Most improper," Rajaratnam had warned her. "Only master tailors may speak with distinguished gentlemen."

Rajaratnam chewed his *bhatura*. "What is that?" he said, pointing to the bundle under Navita's arm.

"It's fabric for a sari," said Navita. "It's for my mother's birthday. I was hoping I could keep it here, rather than at home, so she doesn't see it."

"Very well," murmured Rajaratnam, turning back to his receipts. "My sister is indeed lucky to have a dutiful child who buys her birthday gifts. But keep it well away from my bolts of expensive cloth. I don't want any strands of cheap fabric to rub off onto them."

Navita went downstairs into the cellar room, leaving Rajaratnam to his *bhatura* and his receipts.

2 Chalk and Charcoal

The bolts of expensive woollen cloth, stacked in tidy rows against the cellar walls, trapped the heat beneath the front room like rows of pinstriped insulation. Navita could feel beads of sweat forming on her forehead. She put the sari material on top of a set of cupboards in the corner of the room and patted her brow with a handkerchief. A single drop on the expensive material would have Rajaratnam in fits of fury at the ruination of his precious cloth.

On the cutting table in the middle of the cellar lay a sheaf of pale yellow papers, detailing the morning's orders with careful measurements. Navita read Rajaratnam's handwriting carefully. Every Monday, Rajaratnam would gather up his receipts and wave them at his staff.

"Not a scrap of cloth is to be wasted," he said. "How is an honest tailor to make a living with wasteful staff like you?" Navita's job was to ensure that Rajaratnam did, somehow, manage to make a living, by marking out the cloth as exactly as she could.

She unravelled a roll of tissue paper on the cutting table and measured out the dimensions Rajaratnam had written down. Pieces for one suit jacket, one waistcoat and one pair of trousers. Then she cut the shapes of each piece of the suit from the tissue paper, double-checking each measurement as she went.

Finally, after two hours of careful measuring and cutting, Navita took a heavy bolt of cloth from its place along the wall – Super 150 worsted Italian merino, solid charcoal. Super 150 was Rajaratnam's most popular fabric, one hundred and fifty fine threads per inch. She unrolled the soft, dark grey material across the cutting table and arranged the pieces of tissue paper over the expanse of cloth.

"Not a scrap of cloth," echoed Rajaratnam's voice in her mind. Navita tried to arrange the tissue pieces as closely as she could. Satisfied that she could not save Rajaratnam another thread of Super 150, she reached for her chalk. She drew the outlines of the tissue shapes on the charcoal fabric beneath.

At last, she was done. She collected the tissue paper templates, and put them in the bin. The swathe of charcoal Super 150 looked like a large jigsaw puzzle, each piece outlined in chalk and fitting snugly with its neighbour. Now it was up to the cutter, Murugan, to guide his scissors around her chalk lines when he arrived at work for the night shift. Navita was never allowed to actually cut the cloth. She was only a chalk girl. Rajaratnam's rules of properness would never allow such a thing. She could only watch as Murugan wielded his scissors.

Navita tidied away her chalk and rulers and checked that everything was left as Murugan would expect it when he turned up that night. Then she climbed the stairs up to the front room.

"The Super 150, solid charcoal, is ready for the cutter," she told Rajaratnam. Once she had gone, she knew the tailor would head straight downstairs to cast a mournful eye over the gaps between her chalk lines. He would find little to complain about – but she also knew that wouldn't stop him. That, too, was part of the tradition at Rajaratnam S/O Govindarajan.

"*Poy vittu varugiren*," she said. "Goodbye."

"*Poy vittu varugiren*," nodded Rajaratnam. "Don't be late tomorrow. The forecast is for cooler breezes. That means the market will be busy. I feel it in my bones."

Navita nodded and opened the pale green door. Tomorrow was Saturday. It was always

Rajaratnam's busiest day for orders. Once Murugan had finished his night shift and the cutting table was free, she would return for work in the morning.

The hawkers in the laneways were pulling their racks of saris and scarves inside their stalls. Navita thought of the sari she'd hidden away for her mother, a beautiful swatch of vibrant apricot and orange, flecked with gold, adorned with intricately embroidered elephants and palms. Hoping her mother would like the gift, she turned for home.

"Pinstripes and solid charcoals," sighed Navita to her mother, Dana. "Always boring pinstripes and solids. People come to Little India where vibrant colours and fabrics surround them. Yet they choose solid charcoal, grey, no pattern, no liveliness."

"My brother Rajaratnam knows his customers," replied Dana. "He has told me himself, they are people who work in banks and law offices in cities such as Sydney, London and New York. Sober colours are proper for gentlemen such as these."

"They can buy boring suits in Sydney, London or New York," replied Navita. "Why do they travel all the way to Singapore to buy what they can buy at home? They should be buying something special they can only find in Little India."

Dana shrugged. "Maybe it takes more than two days in those places," she mused. "Bankers and lawyers are busy."

"Navita D/O Dana," said Navita. "When I set up my business as Little India's best female tailor, Navita D/O Dana will specialise in colourful garments. Fine Tailors and Designs of Liveliness for Distinguished Gentlemen."

"I hope you don't talk like this around Rajaratnam," said her mother in alarm. "That would not be at all proper. He may be your uncle, but he will still fire you if he has to."

"Improperness," continued Navita, relishing the idea of owning her own business and eating *bhatura* while her workers scurried around chalking, cutting and sewing. "We will be known around the world for that!"

Dana shook her head. What were they teaching children at school these days? Solid Super 150s, properness and two-day deliveries. That was where the future of tailoring in Little India lay. Everybody knew that.

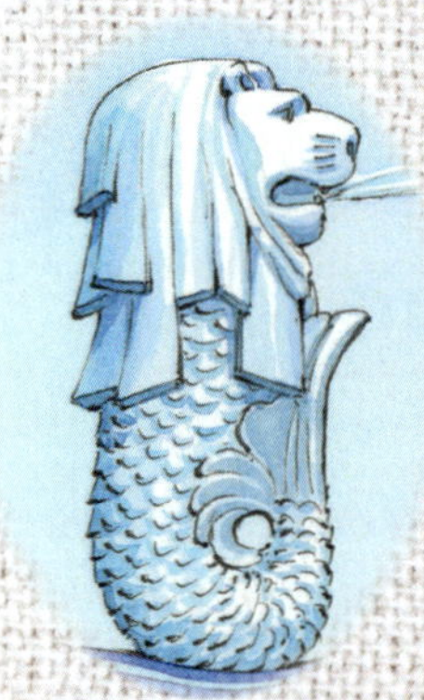

3 The Monsoon Rains

The next morning, Navita let herself in through the pale green door. There, in the front room, stood a beaming Rajaratnam, tape measure draped around his neck. He was exhorting a client to feel the quality of a sample of cloth on his desk. Gone were the receipts and the crumbs of *bhatura*. Rajaratnam was at work. He had found himself a banker in the market.

"This is a fine choice, sir," preened Rajaratnam. "Is it to be for a special occasion?"

"I'm getting married," smiled the client. "I'm stopping over in Singapore on my way to Sydney. I've got friends and business colleagues coming from all over the world."

"Congratulations, sir. And how long are you staying, sir?" asked Rajaratnam.

"Two days," replied the man. "My wedding is next week."

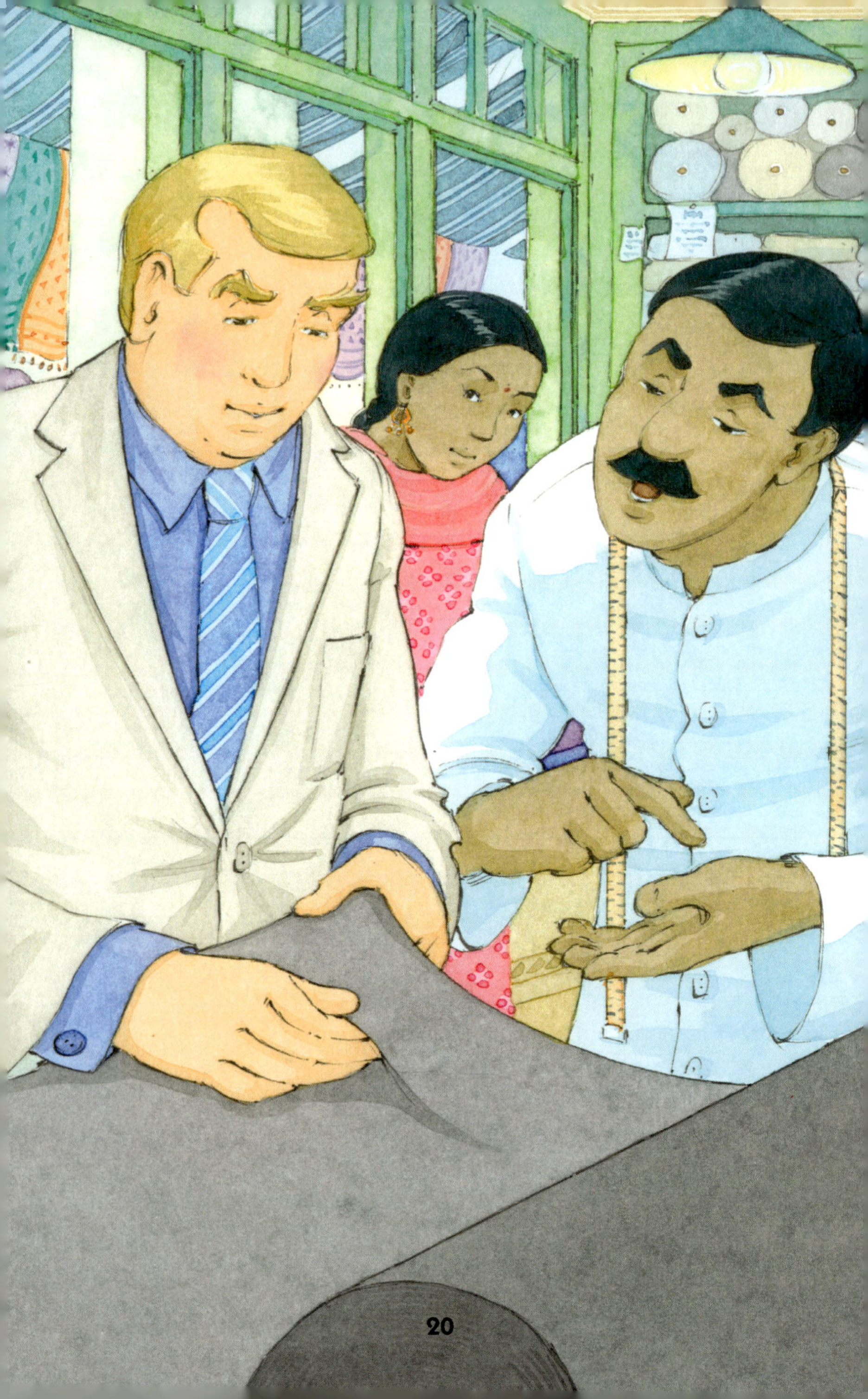

"Excellent, sir. I can guarantee everything will be finished and fitted for you, sir," he smiled. "But if it is to be a wedding suit, sir, may I suggest this cloth instead?" He laid another sample on his desk. "It is a little more expensive, sir, a Super 150 solid charcoal, but feel the quality. Go on, sir, feel the quality."

More grey, sighed Navita, glancing at the sample. Extra-fine merino grey, but still grey. She knew better than to interrupt Rajaratnam with her usual greeting, so she hurried downstairs.

Murugan, who had worked through the night, was cutting the last of the woollen fabric she had laid out the night before.

"*Vanakkã*," she said. Things were less formal downstairs, even though a cutter was always senior to a chalk girl.

"*Vanakkã*," yawned Murugan. "Not too many scraps," he added, pointing to the offcuts on the floor. "The boss will be pleased."

"We'll have a wedding suit soon," said Navita. "Satin lapels and cloth buttons, if Uncle Rajaratnam has his way."

"Excellent," said Murugan, expertly scissoring his way through a panel of cloth. "Charcoal?"

"Charcoal," confirmed Navita resignedly. "I don't know why bankers and lawyers aren't more adventurous."

"Perhaps they are," said Murugan with a wink. "Perhaps they're just like us."

"How?" asked Navita.

"Too scared to say 'no' to your uncle Rajaratnam," chuckled the cutter, with a final snip of his scissors. "Now take these pieces of fabric upstairs to Ovashni. I'm finished. I'm going home to my breakfast and to my bed. I'll see you later when I come back for my afternoon shift."

The client had gone, but Navita could tell by Rajaratnam's smile that he had been successful in his sales pitch. He sat at his desk, scribbling dimensions and instructions on a pale yellow piece of paper. Not wishing to interrupt him, Navita dutifully delivered the fabric pieces to Ovashni.

"*Vanakkã*," she said to Ovashni, who looked up from her sewing machine with a smile.

"*Vanakkã*, Navita," replied Ovashni. "And what do we have here?"

"More charcoal," sighed Navita.

"We are lucky to live in Singapore," laughed Ovashni. "The rest of the world must be so very, very grey."

On her way back downstairs, Rajaratnam waved Navita over and handed her a handful of pale yellow papers.

"Super 150 worsted Italian merino, solid charcoal," he declared with a look of satisfaction. "A fine choice."

"A fine choice," nodded Navita, forcing a smile.

"Not a scrap of cloth is to be wasted," added Rajaratnam. "It's difficult enough for an honest tailor to make a living."

With Murugan gone and the cellar to herself, Navita concentrated on translating Rajaratnam's measurements and instructions, firstly onto her tissue paper and then into chalk outlines, carefully drawn onto the Super 150, solid charcoal.

Suddenly, a low rumble interrupted her thoughts. She looked up from the grey fabric, her head cocked to one side. What was that? Had a truck got lost in the laneways and come grinding to a halt outside the shophouse?

Boom! Navita knew at once that this wasn't a truck. It was thunder, rolling across the island. She turned back to the Super 150. She hoped it was just a passing storm. Splashing home through the puddles of Little India would be no fun. It had been weeks since the last shower, and that just meant more dust and more dirt would be washed off the roofs of the shophouses into muddy puddles in the laneways.

When Murugan finally clattered his way back down the stairs to the cellar, Navita looked at him in alarm. He was soaking wet. This wasn't just a passing shower.

"Find me a towel, Navita," he said, dripping water onto the floor. "If any of this splatters onto the fabric, Rajaratnam will have a fit."

Underneath the sari material she had hidden for her mother, Navita found Murugan a towel. "It's the monsoon," said the cutter, rubbing his hair and face. "I'm sure it is. It's come early."

"I heard the thunder," said Navita. "It's been crashing all morning."

"It's kept me awake all day," complained Murugan. "I should have been sleeping. And rain," he added, using the towel to brush as much water as he could off his tunic. "I've never seen so much rain in October. It's up to my ankles in some parts."

"I've marked out the Super 150 for the wedding suit," said Navita, pointing at the table. She looked at her watch. "I should be going. I have chores to do at home."

"*Apram paarkalame,*" said Murugan, picking up his scissors and casting an expert cutting eye over the swathe of solid charcoal Super 150. "See you later."

As Navita climbed the stairs up to the front room, she had no idea that it would be much, much later than anyone expected. The monsoon would see to that.

4 Disaster and Opportunity

Throughout the afternoon, and all through the night, the early monsoon rain grew heavier and heavier. Sheets of water fell from the roofs of the shophouses, and the laneways, unable to cope with the rain, filled with muddy water. The next morning, Navita splashed her way across Serangoon Road, finding a brief respite from the monsoon in the covered market. Tourists had deserted the intersection of the four laneways.

Almost all of the traders had decided to close for the rest of the weekend. One or two stood huddled in bedraggled groups, bemoaning the lack of trade. No one in his or her right mind, not even a tourist, would venture out in this weather.

Navita forded the puddles across the laneway to the pale green door. The water was almost up to the second step. She turned the handle and stepped inside. Rajaratnam was sitting at his desk, cradling his head in his hands, a look of despair on his face. An uneaten *bhatura* lay on his desk.

"What am I to do?" he wailed, looking up at Navita. "A few showers and my cutter deserts me. How can I meet my two-day deadline now?"

For once, Navita forgot her formal greeting. "What's going on, uncle?" she asked instead.

"How is an honest tailor to make a living, with ungrateful staff like mine?" moaned Rajaratnam pitifully. "Murugan gets a phone call from his wife, telling him their whole district is flooded and his children are stranded at some daycare centre, and what does he do? Finish his cutting, like any good cutter would? No! He cuts the jacket and trousers, hands them to Ovashni and goes off to rescue his wife and children! He deserts me and tells me he will finish the waistcoat this afternoon. But I have my client coming in this afternoon!"

"That is only because he knows you are such a fair and honourable man," said Navita, after a moment's careful thought. "I imagine he thinks that rescuing his wife and children from floods is the proper thing to do."

"Yes, yes," agreed Rajaratnam hurriedly. "I am indeed very fair and honourable. Some would say too fair and too honourable. But it will be my undoing. It is now day two of my two-day guarantee. How will I get my suit cut in time?"

Navita took a deep breath. "It's only the waistcoat," she said. "I will cut it."

"You?" gasped Rajaratnam. "But you are just a chalk girl. No, no, no. That would be most improper."

"I've watched Murugan cut fabrics almost every day for the last two years," said Navita confidently. "I'm sure I know what to do. And anyway, there is no one else to do it. Ovashni will be busy sewing the jacket and trousers. And you must continue your important master tailoring in the front room."

"Yes," agreed Rajaratnam reluctantly. He eyed his *bhatura* hungrily. "A captain must not abandon his ship. And I have many important receipts I must attend to. Very well. You may cut the waistcoat. But be very careful. Not a scrap of cloth is to be wasted!"

Navita did her very best to suppress the grin she could feel welling up inside her until she reached the stairs down to the cellar. At last! She was to be allowed the task of actually cutting fabric! Safely out of Rajaratnam's sight, she allowed a huge smile to spread across her face. At the top of the stairs, she reached for the light switch and flicked it on.

Her smile vanished.

She crept down the stairs, surveying the scene in front of her. Starting in the thundery skies of Singapore, a torrent of water had fallen on the roof of the shophouse. It had been channelled down hundred-year-old tiles, drains

and guttering. The volume of the water had overwhelmed the drains and gutters. Water had trickled down the old walls, collected under the floors, and worked its way lower and lower, until it found the old ceiling of the cellar. There, it had pooled until it finally seeped through the old wood. Drop by wood-stained drop, it had fallen onto the cutting table – and into the Super 150 finest Italian merino that would now never be turned into a waistcoat.

Worse was to come. Navita gasped when she saw the water cascading down the plaster wall behind the bolts of expensive cloth. At the base of each column of cloth, a dark water stain was working its way up the fabric.

Within seconds, Navita's dream of becoming a cutter was dashed. The charcoal Super 150 was ruined. And until they dried, the other bolts were just as useless. There was nothing to cut. Worse still, Rajaratnam would explode when he learnt

that he could not fulfil his client's order. It would be the first time since 1964 that Rajaratnam S/O Govindarajan had failed in its promise to deliver within two days.

Navita looked around the cellar, wondering how she was going to tell Rajaratnam of this disaster. She was about to climb up the stairs and break the news, when her eyes fell upon something on top of the cupboard in the corner. Her mother's sari material. She ran over and felt the package. It was still dry. She turned and headed for the stairs. At least it was not all bad. Her mother would still have her birthday sari.

And then Navita stopped.

Like the monsoon rains, seeping unseen into the cellar, an idea suddenly burst into her mind. She turned back towards the cutting table. She retrieved the tissue paper templates from the bin beneath it. And she began work.

An hour later, Ovashni couldn't believe her eyes. "Has Rajaratnam lost his mind?" she blurted out, when she saw the panels of cut fabric that Navita laid on her sewing table.

"Not yet," replied Navita. "But he's about to lose a client if he doesn't have a jacket, trousers and waistcoat ready by this afternoon."

Ovashni shrugged her shoulders.

"Well," she said, "it'll be on your head. I just do the sewing. It's been nice working with you, Navita."

5 Most Improper

Rajaratnam's glum look transformed itself into a beaming smile the moment the bell on the pale green door tinkled. He stood up, adjusted the tape measure draped around his neck and bowed politely to the client. "Welcome back, sir," he said. "Terrible weather, isn't it? Luckily, not even a monsoon in October can stop Rajaratnam S/O Govindarajan meeting our two-day guarantee. I do believe your wedding suit is ready as promised."

Rajaratnam pressed a small button on his desk and, in the room above them, a small bell tinkled. Navita appeared, carrying a suit bag that was fully zipped up. It was another of Rajaratnam's rules of properness. "One must keep the client in anticipation until the very last moment," the master tailor always insisted. "Fine suits for

distinguished gentlemen must never be displayed, but must instead be revealed."

"Aha!" said Rajaratnam, as he swept the suit bag out of Navita's hands and hung it on a rack. He was so intent on the suit that he didn't notice Navita's nervous eyes, glancing anxiously at the client.

"And now, sir, I am pleased to present to you, a fine suit crafted in the time-honoured tradition of Rajaratnam S/O Govindarajan!" declared Rajaratnam proudly, With a flourish, he unzipped the suit bag, his twinkling eyes fixed on the client's face, waiting for a reaction.

"Wow!" said the client. With a satisfied look, Rajaratnam nodded and turned to examine the contents of the suit bag himself. When he saw what was inside, he looked as if he had been struck with a bolt of lightning from the monsoon thunderstorm.

"Wow!" repeated the client, admiring the wedding suit. Rajaratnam's mouth went up and down, but not a sound came out. He was flabbergasted at what he saw.

"I've never seen anything like it," said the client, reaching out to touch the waistcoat. Its intricately embroidered elephants and palms in vibrant apricot, orange and gold were perfectly framed by the charcoal of the jacket and trousers.

"Neither have I," croaked Rajaratnam, finally finding his voice.

"It's beautiful," said the client. "I'm delighted you didn't do it in charcoal."

Rajaratnam gulped and nodded. Every tradition instilled in him since 1964 dictated that the client was always right. Under the circumstances, it would have been most improper to disagree. Most improper.

"If your poor mother Dana were not my sister, I would be forced to dismiss you instantly," hissed Rajaratnam once the satisfied client had left. "Now get down to that cellar. I don't want to see you for the rest of the day."

When Murugan finally returned to work later in the afternoon, he listened with wide-eyed horror at what had happened while he was selfishly rescuing his wife and children.

"It is, I suppose, all my fault," muttered Rajaratnam darkly, as he shook his head in despair. "My generosity in giving you time off to rescue your wife and children was too fair and too honourable. And, as I feared, fairness and honour will be my undoing."

As soon as the monsoon rains stopped, the hawkers once again filled the laneways with their racks of saris and scarves. Navita, having used the apricot and orange sari fabric to make the waistcoat, found another piece, just as lively and colourful, for her mother's birthday present. Rajaratnam spent the next few days filling out insurance claims for his damaged materials, and repairing his wounded pride with receipts and *bhatura*. And then, just as the horrific memory of apricot and orange coloured elephants and palms was starting to fade, the phone calls began. The first was from Sydney.

"Yes, yes, I am indeed the tailor who made your friend's wedding suit," sighed Rajaratnam. He was about to launch into a well-rehearsed apology when a look of surprise came across his face. "Well, yes, sir, I suppose I could manage that. But may I suggest a Super 150 solid charcoal instead, sir? It is a little more expensive but ... no?

OK, sir, I understand. Of course, sir, I can manage that. Yes, I can deliver worldwide."

He scribbled some notes on a pale yellow slip of paper. Then the phone rang again. This time it was London.

No sooner had Rajaratnam put down the phone than it rang again. New York. He scribbled and scribbled. He couldn't believe it. Never in all his years as a master tailor had he imagined that something like this might happen.

The next afternoon found Rajaratnam sitting behind his desk, chewing disconsolately on his *bhatura*. He stared at the slips of yellow paper that covered his desk. He had to make a decision. He was a businessman as well as a master tailor, and he knew what he had to do. This was going to be awkward, but it had to be done. The future reputation of Rajaratnam S/O Govindarajan, Master Tailors and Alterations for Distinguished Gentlemen, depended upon it.

The pale green door opened and the bell tinkled. Her eyes downcast, Navita walked into the front room.

"*Madhiya vanakkam*, Uncle," murmured Navita as she walked past. "Good afternoon."

Rajaratnam stood up. "*Madhiya vanakkam*," he replied. "Please come over here, Navita. I have something I need to discuss with you."

Navita's heart sank. She knew her uncle was still angry with her for making the waistcoat out of sari material. Maybe he'd finally decided to get rid of her.

"You must understand, Navita, that what I am about to say gives me enormous pain. It is not easy for me to do this."

Navita gulped. Her mother had warned her that, even though he was her uncle, he would still fire her if he wanted to.

"Rajaratnam S/O Govindarajan has a fine tradition," continued Rajaratnam. "One that I have built up since 1964. But, as a clever businessman, I always have to be on the lookout for threats to my business."

"I'm sorry, Uncle," murmured Navita. "I was just trying to do something a little different ... a little more lively."

Rajaratnam held up his hand. "My mind is made up," he said. "As of this morning, Rajaratnam S/O Govindarajan will no longer require your services as a chalk girl."

Navita knew there was no point arguing. She stood up to leave.

"Where are you going?" said Rajaratnam. "I said I don't require your services as a chalk girl. But I do need your services as a Designer of Lively Accessories for Distinguished Gentlemen."

Now it was Navita's turn to be speechless. She stared at her uncle. Had she heard correctly – a designer?

Rajaratnam waved his hand at the pile of pale yellow orders he had taken from the phone calls that morning. "Much as I hate to admit it, it has become clear to me that the traditions of 1964 are no longer the traditions of today's distinguished gentlemen. And one of the threats to my business is that it fails to move with the times. There are a hundred other tailors out there in Little India who can sew charcoal suits in two days. But there are none who have the flair and foresight to offer something truly unique – bespoke hand-tailored waistcoats to enliven even the greyest of people."

"You mean I can design waistcoats?" said Navita. "Colourful waistcoats? Lively waistcoats?"

"Your pay will be the same," added Rajaratnam hurriedly. "I can't have everyone thinking I have been overly fair and honourable."

"Thank you, Uncle," smiled Navita. "I don't know what to say."

"Well, I do," said Rajaratnam. "Get to work! You have material to find and international orders to fulfil."

He handed over the pile of pale yellow order slips. Navita flipped through them. Cerise. Scarlet. Turquoise. Gold and sapphire. Not a charcoal grey to be seen.

Rajaratnam stood up. "I have to go and find some bankers or lawyers," he said, heading for the door. "Let's just hope that the market is teeming with them this morning."

Navita followed her uncle through the pale green door. She turned left in search of materials and he turned right in search of customers.

"And Navita," called Rajaratnam, as he crossed the road.

"Yes, Uncle?" said Navita. She was sure her uncle was about to thank her for helping Rajaratnam S/O Govindarajan move with the times.

"Not a scrap of cloth is to be wasted," he said. "We are still honest tailors and we need to make a living!"

Navita nodded and headed towards the racks of saris she could see further down the laneway. "Some things never change," she thought.

It was only after she started laying out her chalk and her tissue paper that she gradually realised what her uncle had said.

We. *We* are honest tailors.

It was the best compliment that a master tailor could have given to a lowly chalk girl from Little India.